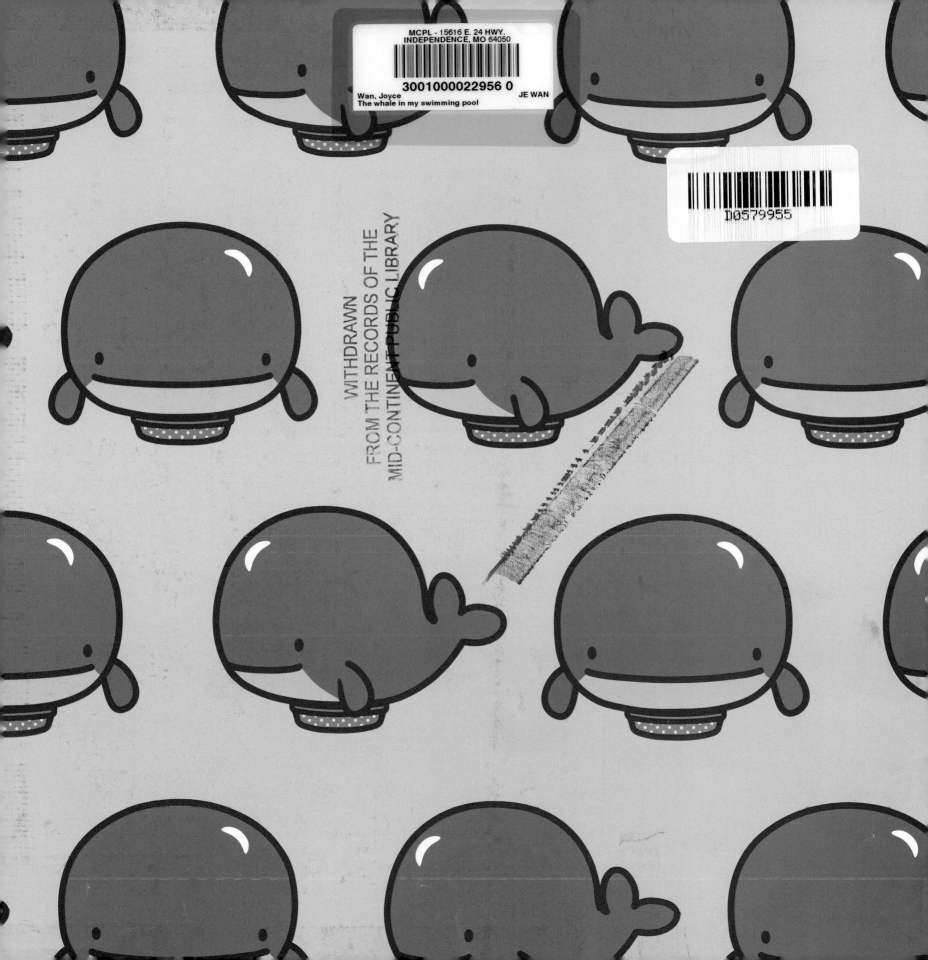

For Maddy and Brook,

who always help me see

the silly side of things —J.W.

Farrar Straus Giroux Books for Young Readers
175 Fifth Avenue, New York 10010

Color separations by Embassy Graphics Ltd.
Printed in China by RR Donnelley Asia Printing Solutions Ltd.,
Dongguan City, Guangdong Province
First edition, 2015
3   5   7   9   10   8   6   4   2

mackids.com

Library of Congress Cataloging-in-Publication Data
Wan, Joyce, author, illustrator.
    The whale in my swimming pool / Joyce Wan. — First edition.
       pages cm
    Summary: A young boy discovers a whale in his pool and tries everything
he can think of to get it out.
    ISBN 978-0-374-30037-1 (hardback)
    ISBN 978-0-374-30188-0 (board book)
    [1. Whales—Fiction.   2. Swimming pools—Fiction.]   I. Title.

PZ7.W1788Wh 2015
[E]—dc23

2014041144

Farrar Straus Giroux Books for Young Readers may be purchased for
business or promotional use. For information on bulk purchases please contact
Macmillan Corporate and Premium Sales Department at (800) 221-7945 x5442
or by email at specialmarkets@macmillan.com.

THE WHALE IN MY SWIMMING POOL

Joyce Wan

Farrar Straus Giroux · New York

Race you to the pool!

Whoa . . .
A whale?!

Moooooom, there's a whale in my swimming pool.

Great, honey. Don't forget about sunscreen.

Sunscreen? On a whale?

Okay, I'm going to close my eyes and count to ten, and when I'm done, you'd better be gone!
Ready?

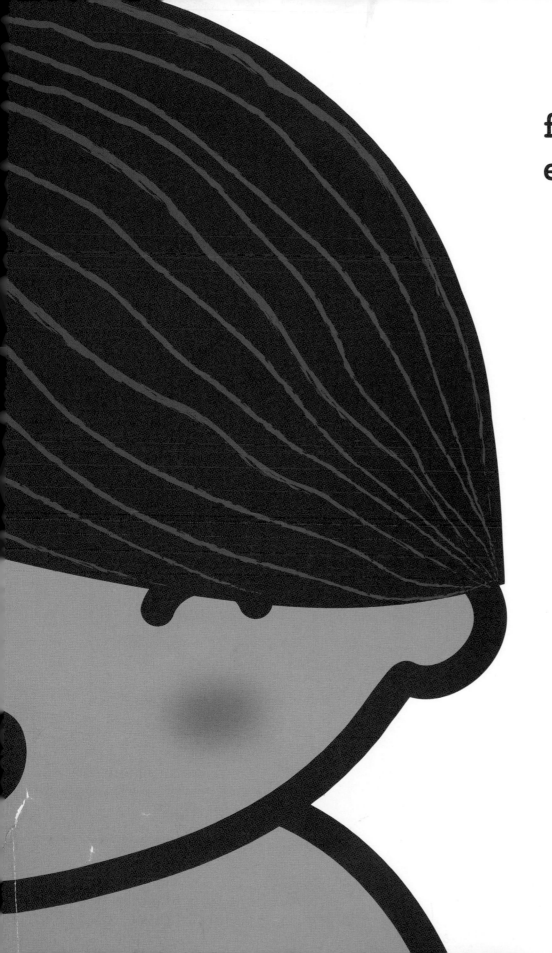

One, two, three,
four, five, six, seven,
eight, nine . . .

Ten!

Ugh!

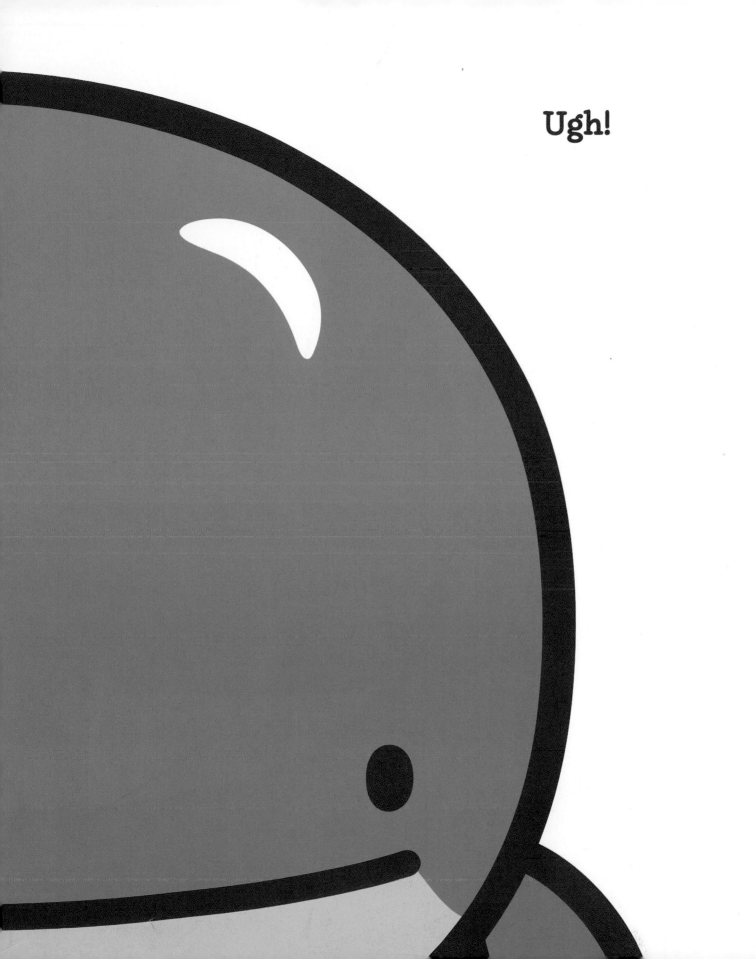

Maybe you just
need a little help.

Why *my* pool?
Why not the pool next door?
They have the best pool on the block!

How about a game?
Fetch!

Here fishy, fishy, fishy.

Wouldn't you rather
swim with other whales?

I'll give you my
allowance.

What if we take turns?

Tag! You're it!

How will I ever get this
whale out of my pool?

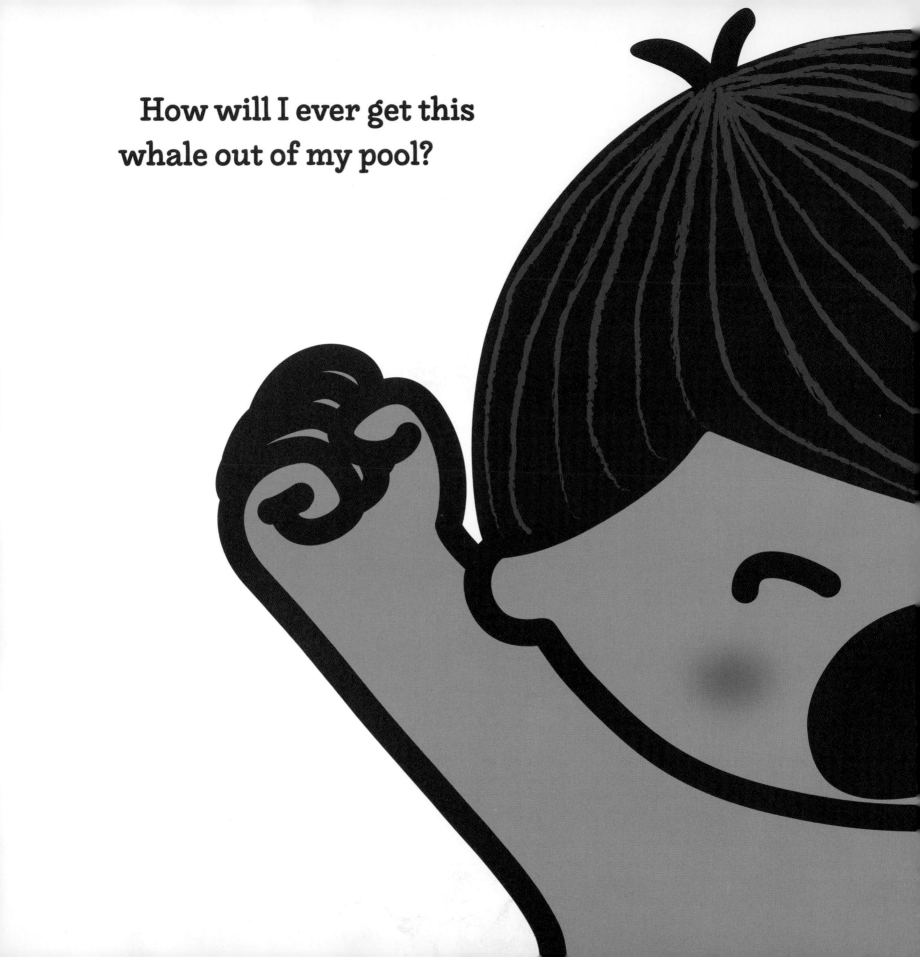

I'll never get to go swimming ever again!

 I give up.

Wait a minute. I have an idea!

Wait here. I'll be right back.

Well, maybe this is not *so* bad after all.

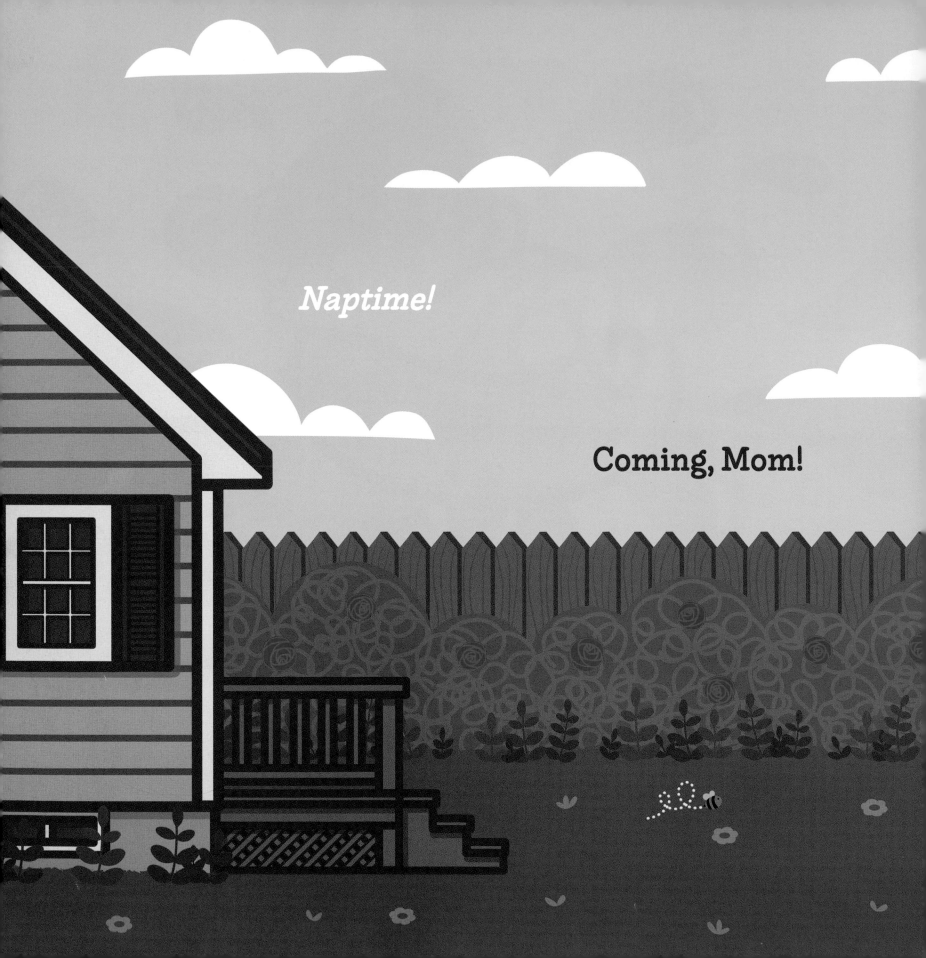

Oh, great.
He snores!